THE · NIGHT BEFORE · CHRISTMAS

BY
CLEMENT · C · MOORE · LL·D ·

I LLUSTRATED · BY
ARTHUR · RACKHAM

WEATHERVANE BOOKS · NEW YORK

A NOTE ON THE ILLUSTRATOR

ARTHUR RACKHAM, in his navy blue suit with stiff white collar and blue and white spotted bowtie, was the leading English illustrator of the day by the age of 43. After his death in 1939 a London *Sunday Times* article described him as having "an elusive sense of humor that showed itself in a twinkling eye and a dry smile." Certainly he put the humor to use in *The Night Before Christmas:* it is he matching twinkling smiles with Santa before the hearth in the frontispiece.

Rackham's life and career were as unspectacular as his art is brilliant. He was a kindly, unpretentious, very hard working man whose fantasies were played out for all the world to see. Born in 1867 of a typical middle-class Victorian family, he was proud to be a cockney. He showed a precocious talent for drawing as a child, and later said that he was committed to watercolors from "the first day when I was given, as all little boys are, a shilling paint-box....this craft has been my constant companion."

He sent occasional contributions to illustrated papers at the start of his career; the first drawings appeared in *Scraps* of October, 1884. He painted watercolors during this time, and later joined the staff of the *Westminster Budget*, where he was prominently featured for three years. His drawings of well-known contemporary figures, including the Queen and Mr. Gladstone, became a regular feature. From 1893 on he became increasingly occupied with book illustration; a travel book of the United States done from photos was one of the first. By the end of the century he had made his mark as an illustrator. Particular influences on his style may be found in Cruikshank, Caldecott, Dicky Doyle, Arthur Boyd Houghton, the artists of Germany and Japan, and the art of Aubrey Beardsley. It is certain that he, in turn, influenced many others, including Walt Disney.

Rip Van Winkle, published in 1905, established Rackham as the foremost decorative illustrator of the Edwardian period. His last illustrations, and a longtime ambition, were done for *The Wind in the Willows.*

His work for *The Night Before Christmas* is an example of his thorough knowledge of the texts he illustrated and his fidelity to the author's meaning. Never guilty of the slavish interpretation, however, Rackham was a poetic craftsman whose imagination was to change the world of book illustration, and surely the worlds of those lucky enough to open to a page and find his work upon it.

—Patricia Horan

A NOTE ON THE AUTHOR

Dr Clement C. Moore, the author of these verses, was born in the city of New York in 1779. The son of Bishop Benjamin Moore, he became a well-known classical scholar, and in 1821 was appointed Professor of Hebrew and Greek Literature in the Protestant Episcopal Seminary in New York. He died in 1863. Among his contributions to literature and learning is a monumental "Hebrew and English Lexicon," a work of great labour and the product of many years' toil. Yet, strangely enough, Dr Moore's fame to-day rests almost solely on this poem, which he wrote one Christmas-time for his children. Published first under the title "A Visit from St Nicholas," it has been translated into nearly all European languages, and has even been issued in Braille.

PLATES IN COLOUR

THE NIGHT

BEFORE

CHRISTMAS

'TWAS the night before Christmas, when all through the house
Not a creature was stirring, not even a mouse;
The stockings were hung by the chimney with care,
In hopes that St Nicholas soon would be there;

THE children were nestled all snug in their beds,
While visions of sugar-plums danced in their heads;
And Mamma in her kerchief, and I in my cap,
Had just settled our brains for a long winter's nap,

The children were nestled all snug in their beds

W HEN out on the lawn there arose such a clatter,
I sprang from the bed to see what was the matter.
Away to the window I flew like a flash,
Tore open the shutters and threw up the sash.

THE moon on the breast of the new-fallen snow
Gave the lustre of midday to objects below,
When, what to my wondering eyes should appear,
But a miniature sleigh, and eight tiny reindeer,

It must be St Nick

With a little old driver, so lively and quick,
I knew in a moment it must be St Nick.
More rapid than eagles his coursers they came,
And he whistled, and shouted, and called them by name :

Now, *Dasher*! now, *Dancer*! now, *Prancer* and *Vixen*!
On, *Comet*! on, *Cupid*! on, *Donner* and *Blitzen*!
To the top of the porch! to the top of the wall!
Now dash away! dash away! dash away all!"

As dry leaves that before the wild hurricane fly,
When they meet with an obstacle, mount to the sky,
So up to the house-top the coursers they flew,
With the sleigh full of Toys, and St Nicholas too.

AND then, in a twinkling, I heard on the roof
The prancing and pawing of each little hoof.
As I drew in my head, and was turning around,
Down the chimney St Nicholas came with a bound.

HE was dressed all in fur, from his head to his foot,
And his clothes were all tarnished with ashes and
  soot;
A bundle of Toys he had flung on his back,
And he looked like a pedlar just opening his pack.

H<small>IS</small> eyes—how they twinkled! his dimples how merry!
His cheeks were like roses, his nose like a cherry!
His droll little mouth was drawn up like a bow,
And the beard of his chin was as white as the snow;

Filled all the stockings

THE stump of a pipe he held tight in his teeth,
And the smoke it encircled his head like a wreath;
He had a broad face and a little round belly,
That shook when he laughed, like a bowlful of jelly.

H E was chubby and plump, a right jolly old elf,
And I laughed when I saw him, in spite of myself;
A wink of his eye and a twist of his head
Soon gave me to know I had nothing to dread.

HE spoke not a word, but went straight to his work,
And filled all the stockings; then turned with a jerk,
And laying his finger aside of his nose,
And giving a nod, up the chimney he rose;

HE sprang to his sleigh, to his team gave a whistle,
And away they all flew like the down of a thistle.
But I heard him exclaim, ere he drove out of sight,

HAPPY CHRISTMAS

TO

ALL

AND

TO ALL

A GOOD NIGHT